THE TRUCKER

Written by
Brenda Weatherby

Illustrated by
Mark Weatherby

SCHOLASTIC INC.
New York   Toronto   London   Auckland   Sydney
Mexico City   New Delhi   Hong Kong   Buenos Aires

Special thanks to Jamie Lowe, Sam Tiemersma, Barbara Witas, Sinead Coleman,
Martha Parlitsis, Perry Sofferman, Haydee Elfanagely, Max Desiano, Kevin Kostka,
and Ellie Berger.

ISBN 0-439-67878-1

12 11 10 9 8 7 6 5 4 3 2 1   4 5 6 7 8 9/0

Printed in the U.S.A.   40

First Scholastic paperback printing, October 2004

The artwork was created with acrylic, sand, and road dirt.
The display text was set in Bodoni Highlight ICG.
The text was set in Souvenir Medium 17 point.
Book design by Yvette Awad

For my Mother,

because she always knew I could

— B. W.

For my Father, "Grandpa,"

and to my son, Wesley,

a third-generation trucker

— M. W.

Early one morning, while Wesley was playing quietly in his room, something odd began to happen to his red semi-flatbed rig.

First it began to rattle and shake.

Then it grew . . . .

and it grew . . . .

and it grew. . . .

"Time for breakfast," Wesley's mom called from the kitchen.
But he didn't hear her. He had work to do.

Wesley bob-tailed down to the yard.
There he found his load all bundled out
and ready to go.
He hitched up the trailers.

Then he carefully looked over each part of the rig.
Brakes — okay. Lights — all working. Hoses — no problem.
One last thump on each tire to check the pressure.
If all went well, he could get to the lumberyard and unload
well before dark.

The truck roared down the street. When Wesley reached
the bus stop, the children were waiting for the school bus.
They gave him the trucker signal. All the truckers know it.
Wesley answered them with a long, loud blast on his air horn.

"PFVVVVVVVVVVVVV!"

The nearby country road was bumpy and bouncy.
Trees and flowers and animals whooshed past.

The highway was not as much fun. It was flat and straight, and it stretched on and on hundreds of miles ahead. Wesley picked up his CB radio for company.

"Anyone out there got your ears on?" he asked.

The radio was full of static. "Can't talk now," said a voice. "Not with this window wash up ahead."

That meant rain was coming.

Wesley turned off the highway and looked up at the darkening clouds. The storm was so close, you could smell it.

A yellow service truck was stuck in a ditch and needed help.
It was no trouble pulling the little truck back onto the road.

Suddenly the wind blew, and the sky blackened.
One big raindrop splattered on the windshield.
Then another. And another. Lighting flashed.
Thunder crashed. The windshield wipers pounded.

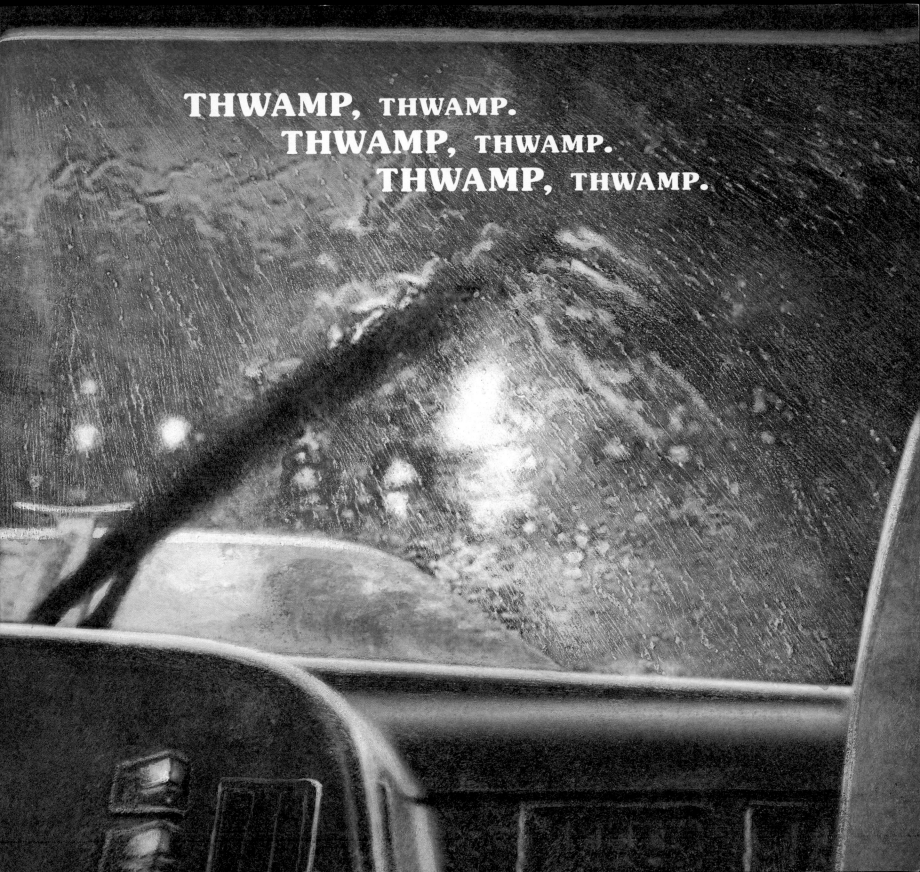

THWAMP, THWAMP.
THWAMP, THWAMP.
THWAMP, THWAMP.

Muddy water splashed against the windows. It was hard to see, and now the roads looked unfamiliar. Wesley was lost.

Then suddenly — **KA-BOOM!**
A sharp tug on the steering wheel told Wesley he had blown a tire.

He pulled over to the side of the road. There was no one around to help. Wesley couldn't fix a big truck like this alone. . . .

He radioed for help.

"Bubble trouble," he called into the CB.

"CRACKLE-CRACKLE-KHHKHKHKH!"

was all the radio could say.

Then, something wonderful happened. The yellow service truck he had helped out of the ditch appeared. When the driver saw that Wesley was in trouble, he pulled over to help him.

When the tire was changed, Wesley thanked
the driver. The driver let Wesley follow him the
rest of the way to the lumberyard.

At last he was there.

But all the excitement made Wesley very sleepy.
He was too sleepy to unload his lumber. His eyelids
were heavy. He couldn't stay awake another
moment.

"Better bag out and get some shut-eye," he told
the radio. Then he pulled off the road to take a nap.
Just as he drifted off into a deep, deep sleep,
the truck began to rattle and shake.

North Fork
Nooksack
River

"Hey, Little Man, dreaming about trucking again?"
Wesley rubbed his eyes and looked around. Today
was the day he was going to work with Daddy.

"You fell asleep in your room before we had to leave,
so I carried you into the truck," Daddy said. "You missed
a big thunderstorm, and we had a nasty flat tire."

Wesley climbed into the front seat and fastened his seat belt. He could hardly wait to spend the whole day with Daddy on the big rig!

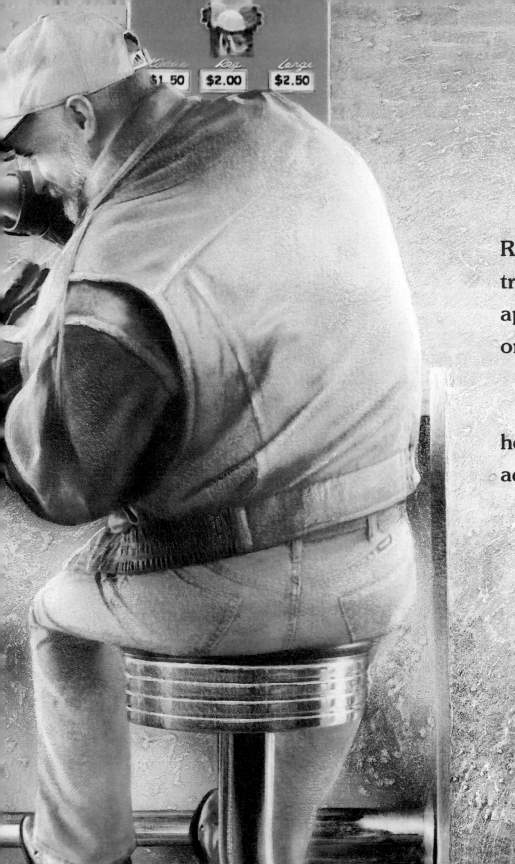

They stopped for lunch at the Road-Hog Truck Stop Cafe. Being a trucker can make a guy work up an appetite. Wesley was so hungry, he ordered two deluxe burgers with fries.

And all the way to the lumberyard, he told Daddy about his exciting adventure as a trucker.

TRUCKER TALK

ALLIGATOR IN THE HAMMER LANE

Big piece of tire in the fast lane

ANYBODY GOT THEIR EARS ON?

Anyone listening on the CB radio?

BETTER BAG OUT AND GET SOME SHUT-EYE

Better leave the channel and get some sleep

BOBTAILING

Driving a semi-flatbed truck without a trailer

BUBBLE TROUBLE

Tire trouble

BUNDLED OUT RIG COMING THROUGH

Heavily loaded truck coming through

CAREFUL ON THE BOARDWALK

Careful on the bumpy roads

DOUBLES

Two trailers hitched together

EAT-EM-UP AT YARDSTICK 157

Truck stop cafe at mile marker 157

FOUR-WHEELER ON THE GRASS NEEDS A DRAGON WAGON

A car on the median strip needs a tow truck

KIDDIE CAR ON THE SIDE

A school bus on the shoulder

SEMI-FLATBED RIG

A semi truck hauling a flatbed trailer

SLEEPER

Bed in back of a truck cab

TAKE THE GRANNY LANE ON THE BOULEVARD

Take the slow lane on the interstate

THERE'S A WINDJAMMER ON THE TIN CAN

There's a chatterbox on the CB radio

THERE'S A WINDOW WASH UP AHEAD

There's a rainstorm up ahead

TRUCK 'EM EASY

Have a safe trip